HORROR

Copyright © 2024 by Kathe Koja

Cover by Daniella Batsheva
Interior design and illustrations by Joel Amat Güell

ISBN: 9781960988294

CLASH Books
Troy, NY

All rights reserved.

This is a work of fiction. Unless otherwise indicated, all the names, characters, businesses, places, events and incidents in this book are either the product of the author's imagination or used in a fictitious manner. Any resemblance to actual persons, living or dead, or actual events is purely coincidental.

No part of this book may be reproduced in any form or by any electronic or mechanical means, including information storage and retrieval systems, without written permission from the author, except for the use of brief quotations in a book review.

HORROR

@clashbooks   @clashbooks   /clashbooks

Email: clashmediabooks@gmail.com

Impreso en Colombia - Printed in Colombia

CATHERINE
THE
GHOST

BY

Kathe Koja

"Koja's voice is arousing, spectral, the voice is moors. Wholly, here: a gothic gift."

—Josh Malerman, New York Times bestselling author of *Bird Box*

"A lush, Gothic re-entry into your favorite dark romance. *Catherine the Ghost* stuns."

—Erika T. Wurth, author of *White Horse*

"A haunting meditation on broken promises and the dark underbelly of love."

—Rae Wilde, author of *Merciless Waters*

"A strange and beautiful ode to gothic literature, *Catherine the Ghost* takes the story of *Wuthering Heights* and turns it on its head in the most dark and devastating way. An absolute must-read."

—Gwendolyn Kiste, author of *Reluctant Immortals*

"Dramatic and remarkably alluring with such a rich sense of poeticism, *Catherine the Ghost* is a literary seance that invokes the restless spirit of Brontë while showcasing the verve and magnificence of one of our finest visionaries: Kathe Koja."

—Eric LaRocca, author of *Things Have Gotten Worse Since We Last Spoke*

"Kathe Koja divinely taps into the hereafter with *Catherine the Ghost*, summoning Wuthering Heights and beckoning Brontë to speak from beyond the veil. What they manifest together is a haunting meditation on love and literature, both for and from, two exquisite texts communing with one another across the centuries."

—Clay McLeod Chapman, author of *What Kind of Mother* and *Ghost Eaters*

"Kathe Koja's *Catherine the Ghost* pays beautiful homage to the classic text, Koja's style conforming to Brontë's so seamlessly a true love is revealed, or perhaps a rivalry. This feels like Koja's heart, vulnerable and exposed."

—Charlene Elsby, author of *Violent Faculties* and *The Devil Thinks I'm Pretty*

This book is dedicated to Emily Brontë
hard to govern any way but her own

CATHERINE
THE
GHOST

One

let me in

let me in

the moors stretch as far as the stars that circle like moths in the great blackness—I have climbed past those vast black crags, past what Heaven is, past the scorn of the angels, back to these moors that hold this night's hissing snow and churning trees, back and back and back to the Heights

my struggle is immense

and I see inside past the grey squares of glass the stone floor, white and smooth, and my little rocking chair, and the bitch dog stretched panting near the fireplace—if only I could feel her warm coat, and that deep coaly heat! everything of me is cold, boundlessly cold, everything to me is the grave

my body knows the peat and the wet and the worms

let me in

let me in

by that fire is a young woman, with yellow curls and a black book—Catherine she is named—and Joseph too, that croaking old dastard Joseph, he is berating her, saying that she is nowt, she will *go right to the devil like your mother afore ye!* but she says she will summon that devil to carry him off instead, she mocks him just as we used to, we flung his detestable pieties back into his face, kicked the holy books he gave us straight into the dog kennel, Joseph will not like what he finds in Hell

and Hareton passes through, silent and rough as an unshorn ram

and he is there

Heathcliff

Heathcliff

he feels me near but he must hear me

Heathcliff

yet a stranger is present too, who is this stranger in my house? the stranger trying to take his leave, but prevented by the snow and the dogs, both furious and unfriendly, and then led sneaking and nerveless up the dark stairs by some servant I know neither—even Nelly would never have done so—that servant bids him hide the candle he carries, her master has odd notions about that chamber

my bedchamber

and our box-bed, if only I could lie there now! the way we did as children then not as children, pressed limb to limb, sharing our warmth and our breath, breathing in the smell of his hair, my hands in his hair so thick and black, his face to mine as we shared the pillow

Heathcliff

and the stranger—how dare this rude interloper? takes my books stowed by the bed, to turn the leaves and read what I wrote there— of the days when this bed and this house, the heather and sky, was our all in all, and we its rightful queen and king, and Hindley our daily villain—as he yawns and gawps like a dunce, then spells aloud what I scratched into the bed-box panels, **Catherine Earnshaw Catherine Heathcliff Catherine Linton,** all our tragedy there in those names

and hearing those names sends a jolt of pain, that fresh old pain, through me again and again till I fairly beat the fir tree by the lattice window, its cones dried like bones by the cold and the wind

as the stranger writhes and twists in the dreams I enter, in those

let me in! let me in!

dreams he breaks the pane of glass between us, exposing his foolish hand, when I seize that hand he cannot withdraw, cannot escape me, he whimpers in his panic *Who are you?*

who am I

I've come home

though to him I am still the child of those books, yet he shows me no kindness, he seeks to break my grip by sawing my wrist against the broken pane, dragged back and forth with terror's industry, my blood runs in his dream until it soaks the bedclothes and *Let me go!* he cries in his fear, I can feel that fear, as slippery as the blood, *let me go if you want me to let you in!* but as soon as I slack my grip *Begone,* he shouts, *I'll never let you in, not if you beg for twenty years!*

it is twenty years I've been a waif for twenty years

as I drive myself with all my strength against that frightened mind, that body cowering in the bed that was ours, my struggle thrusts against the fleshly world, I *will* come in

and he shrieks, and his shriek rouses footsteps in the hallway, his shriek at last opens the door

Heathcliff opens the door

Heathcliff you called me, you call me, do you hear me! Heathcliff!

they may bury me twelve feet deep and throw the church down over

me, but I won't rest till you are with me, I never will

Heathcliff!

and I hear an answering whisper, loud to me as a thunderclap

Heathcliff's whisper

Is anyone here?

Two

She is a woman now, eighteen years old, but she sits silent at this icy, barren window like a captive child; an orphaned child. Her father is dead, has been dead, Papa sighing out his last breath just as he sighed out his life: he had kissed her cheek with slack moist smiling lips, he had said *I am going to her,* to her mother. Her mother died the day she was born—was it in the birthing bed, in blood and pain, or after? Papa would never speak of that, and Ellen will not say—Papa always marking his great loss on that day, but never his gain of a daughter, every year a trip to the churchyard, carrying flowers to place beside the headstone half-covered in heath; she never asked to accompany him, she knew she was not wanted there. Did he weep, and pray? Did he tell her she had a daughter, a fine grown daughter? Every other day she was his "angel" and "queen," but never on that day . . . *I am going to her.*

And she knows, now, about death: Papa is gone, and Linton is gone, Linton so briefly her husband, how strange to think of Linton so! Linton with his fair hair and blue eyes, he looked more like Papa than she does . . . she once believed Linton was her friend, then her love, dreaming of him, smuggling him letters, a sweetheart's yearning letters, through the dairy-boy; Mr. Heathcliff read those letters, Mr. Heathcliff wrote the answers. How that shamed her, when she learned of it! and how dreadful that she should have been so utterly deluded; the truest thing about Linton was his death.

That death was nothing like Papa's, except for her presence at the bedside. At first she had begged Mr. Heathcliff to send for a doctor, *I cannot tell how to do, if nobody will help me, he'll die!* believing in a broken way, a way she now can hardly recall, that if somehow she might save Linton, it would be as if she had preserved her father too, preserved something of the life she had known before.

But Mr. Heathcliff only stared at her, that stony black stare, *No one here cares what becomes of him* so no one came, not a doctor, not even Zillah. She was left alone in the parlor with Linton, sponging his wasted face, cleansing him when he voided into the bedclothes, wiping the curdled, sickly mess, his thin body shuddering against the pillows through the long moaning days, the house around her like a world she could no longer enter, then into the deep grave of the nights, Linton's clammy hands twisting in hers, Linton threatening that his father would punish her—punish her how? What could have been worse than those nights?—until very late one night his blue eyes went cloudy as stagnant water, he gagged on frothing blood and sucked for air so she woke Zillah, *Tell Mr. Heathcliff that his son is dying, I'm sure he is this time. Tell him!* But still no one came; death came.

Then she rang the invalid's bell, rang and rang until Mr. Heathcliff entered at last, and bent to the bed—she had never hated anyone before, scarcely believed that she could, yet she had learned hate from Mr. Heathcliff on her last day at the Grange, there in the library below the portrait of her mother, she told him *Nobody loves you! nobody will cry for you when you die!* But in that bleak moment by that bed even her hatred was so numbed she could barely rouse herself to answer when he asked, *Now Catherine, how do you feel?*

I feel and see only death. I feel like death!

Zillah gave her wine, then, red and sour and warm, and Hareton stared at her through his dark tangled hair, and Joseph took Linton away, what had been Linton. And she lay for a week, a fortnight, in that stale carpeted parlor, sleeping to nightmares, waking to silence, as Zillah came and went leaving porridge and water, she nearly asked Zillah about the funeral, but what could it matter? Linton was dead and she was a widow.

And to be widowed in *this* place, this house—where she lives her days hated by Mr. Heathcliff, disliked by Hareton, avoided by Zillah, insulted by Joseph; last night Joseph proclaimed she would go right to the devil like her mother before her, Joseph and his hateful pieties! so she threatened to hex him, curse him off the earth, if only she could— here at the Heights that is hers yet not hers, nothing here is hers, not a spoon or a cup or a parsnip peeling, not the dogs or the horses, the throaty drafts or the warmth of the kitchen, the black shadowy trees and white sunlight past the grey mullioned windows. She can see across the snowy billow of the moors from these windows, and Penistone Crags beyond, but she may not go there, is fully forbidden to go; she recalls saying once to Ellen, laughing at Ellen, *The Grange is not a prison, and you are not my jailer,* she had no understanding then, what it means to be truly confined—if only she could go! if only she had her pony again, dear Minny, or even the pretty bay mare in the stable, she has seen Hareton groom that mare until she shines. That horse, this house, this place is less his than hers, but Hareton rides any horse he chooses, he may go to Gimmerton if he chooses, he may go wherever he wishes to go.

Yet she alone enters the room where no one is permitted to enter, not Hareton nor Joseph nor even Zillah to tidy or refresh, the bedchamber with the oak box bed and its series of names scratched into the paint—no one sees her, she is careful, and who else could have a better right to be there? She knows whose room that is, whose names.

Though last night, in secret, Zillah sent the visitor, Mr. Lockwood, into that room—Mr. Lockwood is the tenant at the Grange, another house that is hers yet not hers; last night she had voiced her wish that Mr. Heathcliff should never find another tenant, till the Grange is a ruin—she watched Zillah do it, watched the candlelight disappear behind that dusty door. And she did not sleep, she lay listening, until Mr. Lockwood woke the rest of the household with his panicked shouts, *Let me go, let me go! Begone!* and sent Mr. Heathcliff into that room in a rage, shouting *What can you mean by talking in this way! How dare you, under my roof!*

And when Mr. Lockwood had been driven shuffling down the

stairs, she listened still, she heard Mr. Heathcliff still in that room, his broken noises as if he wept, can Mr. Heathcliff weep? Mr. Heathcliff saying with a dreadful painful urgency *Come in! come in! Cathy—once more!*

Her mother's portrait from the Grange hangs here now, it almost seems better to belong here. She does not resemble her mother at all, except perhaps her eyes, her gaze . . . Catherine Earnshaw, Catherine Heathcliff, Catherine Linton, her mother's name was Cathy, Catherine, like her own.

Three

the body does not hold me

my body

I can view it, laid between the groping roots in the churchyard like something planted too deep to grow, eyes closed, heart stilled, gown rotted, bare flesh preserved by the peat, its passions only an echo, like a cry in an empty room

the body is the house of grief—it knows the gush of tears, the thin taste of whey served with a slap, the freezing air of the Sunday garret, the helpless furious inner clench of watching the whip rise and fall, rise and fall, the sudden stink of death uncovered in the fields, the velvet cold of a coverlet folded on a colder bed

yet the body is the home of pleasure too, so many pleasures! to wake from sleep, every limb warm and eager to move, to breathe the drenched and freshened air after a rainstorm has passed, press the glossy orange nub of a rosehip to taste its pink paste, feel the deep heat of a coal fire, the slither of silk, the sweet itch and prickle of hay, the bliss of lying lip to lip and skin to skin, heart to pounding heart

all of that is no longer mine

I never dreamed how it might be, to leave the body's house

but there are benefits

hearing I still have, such as no living ears may claim—their voices are available to me, Heathcliff's always, the others whenever I choose, every muttered syllable and whispered thought. I can hear it—and sight, I can see from the boiling edge of eternity to every place my body once roamed, everything my hands once touched

at the Heights, the cupboard with the old hoops and shuttlecocks, mine and Hindley's, Hindley's all split and ruined as he ruined everything he owned—Hindley could hurt us, thrash and curse us, but he could never ruin us, he was never our master—and the heavy chair where my father used to rest, the kitchen and the settle where Nelly would sit and nurse Hareton, Nelly sits there now with her endless mending and her silent thoughts

and the yard and stable where old Joseph shuffles through his chores, and Hareton saddles a pretty mare beside the racks of tack and whips, the bench and rough red blanket Heathcliff wrapped in for sleeping, once Hindley had driven him from the house

and my bedchamber, our bed, and my books with the flowers and roots and heather I pressed inside, the spatters and sketches I made, and the bonnets I never wore, the stockings I tore and left for Nelly to mend, the scabs of wax and white moths dried to dust on the windowsill, that years-long dust disturbed only by Heathcliff, only Heathcliff goes into that room

and the fairy-cave under Penistone Crags where he does not go—we hid our childish treasures there, gleaming grouse feathers and lapwing feathers and weasel bones and elf-bolts, and lay to dream and drowse when we were tired from running and climbing in the sun—and the shadowed hole at its heart, the fairy-kirk where we entered together, breathless and elated, wild with kisses, we gave ourselves there, himself to me and me to him, Heathcliff said *No one can ever part us now*

and the great breathing swath of the moors, the heather and rain-swollen beck and moorcocks' nests, that vastness that gave room to our own, and the grassy paths and ancient guidepost pillar carved to shows the ways that one might go, **W.H.** or **G.** or **T.G.**

and Thrushcross Grange, its silent dining room and crimson carpet and glass-drop chandelier that shines like tears, and the chamber I slept in with its black mirror and velvet coverlets and pillows full of pigeon feathers, and the parlor where the windows frame the garden and the park and the valley beyond like a painting of peaceful wealth, that garden where I saw for certain that grief was a path

and Gimmerton Kirk, where we used to stand beneath the new moon, laughing and daring each other to summon the ghosts to rise from beneath their greening stones and answer our questions of life and death, this churchyard where the heath and blue bilberry grow wild over the wall

Edgar is buried here

I do not see him

perhaps Edgar is in Heaven

Next spring you'll long again to have me under this roof—I told Edgar so, not long before I died—*you'll look back and think you were happy today* but I could never be happy at the Grange, I never was—at times resigned, relieved at least by the absence of Hindley, but more often gloomy, the well-dressed well-kept wife to an agreeable murmuring stranger,

Edgar was always strange to me, like frost to fire, or a drifting leaf to a granite edge, I had more daily satisfaction in the company of my horse, or my dogs, than my husband

my husband

did I care for Edgar? I did, mainly before we wed, he was pleasant, and gave no trouble—but I believed that to marry Edgar would be to place Heathcliff and myself forever safe from Hindley's authority and spite, and free Heathcliff from Hindley's campaign of degradation, the same as if he had fallen into a sucking bog—and such an act could never part *us*, every Linton on the face of the earth might melt into nothing before I would forsake Heathcliff! I believed Heathcliff would learn without needing to be taught the difference between what we were, and what that marriage would be

yet the same day I accepted Edgar, Heathcliff ran off

the same day

I see that day if it happens still, happens always as I watch it

my cautious step downstairs, past Hindley gurgling brandy and curses in his room, to seek out Nelly and tell her my dream—in my living days, dreams came that stayed with me ever after, but this dream, the dream of the rock, went through me like blood through water, it had the hard tang of eternity, it frightened me—yet Nelly turned her back and would not listen, *I won't hear it, Miss, I won't hearken to your dreams!*

so I told instead what I had done, when Edgar came calling, how I gave him my promise to marry, asking if she thought I had done right, answering her dozen questions with all my lesser reasons for that promise, reasons I knew even then were mist in the wind— Edgar was handsome and in love with me, Edgar was rich, I should become the greatest woman of the neighborhood—until Nelly said *As soon as you become Mrs. Linton, Heathcliff loses friend, and love, and all! Have you considered how you'll bear the separation? how he'll bear to be deserted?*

but that was fully imbecilic, I told her so, *Oh that's not what I intend, I shouldn't be Mrs. Linton were such a price demanded! You think me a selfish wretch, but if Heathcliff and I married we would be beggars, if I marry Edgar I can aid Heathcliff to rise*

yet Nelly showed herself as contrary and wearisome as Joseph, Nelly said *You are ignorant of marriage duties, or else you are a wicked girl!* ignorant? who should teach us but ourselves? and wicked, what was her meaning? she could not have known that Heathcliff and I had pledged ourselves already—I was sorry to have asked Nelly, though I had no one else to ask

so I set myself to tell Heathcliff as soon as he came in

but he did not come

he did not come

while I paced waiting from the door to the gate and the gate to the door, stood shouting at the top of the sheepfold as Nelly and Joseph searched through the barn and up the road—Nelly said he must have gone into Gimmerton, Joseph said there was no use searching for anyone on a night so black with storms—and sat watching through those furies of rain, drenched and shivering on the settle, repeating, as if it would call him to me, *Heathcliff Heathcliff*

until the bleak bright sunrise, when Hindley came down haggard but mainly sober, to stand over me and say *You look as dismal as a drowned whelp, what ails you? Were you not with Heathcliff last night? Speak the truth, now*

I never saw Heathcliff last night

You lie, Cathy

And if you do turn him out of doors I'll go with him

as a beggar, as anything, because I knew then, I felt his going like a death inside me and I could not bear it

I could not bear it, my grief shook and throttled me, I beat my fists against the door, the floor, even Nelly was afraid, I saw her eyes roll like a shying horse's

and that grief raised a fever in my body—they said it was a brain fever, they forced me to the bed and bled me, slopped whey and water-gruel at me, Dr. Kenneth said *Take care she does not throw herself downstairs or out of the window, she will not bear crossing anymore*—and I lay in that fever, covered in tears and sweat like a scum of salt, my hands like hot dead animals on the coverlet, until I finally understood that Heathcliff had gone

but did he leave me

we had quarreled that day, before Edgar came, a stupid quarrel, Heathcliff showing me the almanac where he had marked crosses and dots for the days I spent with him and the days I spent with Edgar, though I said he was foolish to do so, said I took no notice, and he insisted *Don't turn me out for those pitiful, silly friends of yours!* so I answered to vex him, *Should I always be sitting with you?*—but he did not see me slap Edgar because I was troubled by our quarrel, did not hear me say to Edgar *I won't be miserable for you!*

yet later Nelly told me that Heathcliff had overheard my talk of marrying, that it was all my fault he had gone, I slapped Nelly so hard my wrist ached

did he leave me? how could he leave me? when he's more myself than I am—if he were annihilated, the Universe would turn to a mighty stranger, but if all else perished and he remained, I should still continue to be—I am—

I am Heathcliff

and I waited for him, I roamed the moors as if I would find him, stood before the fairy-kirk and cried tears like iron for him, wrote letters as if he would read them, while weeks passed, months, with no word, nothing, no sign of where he had gone or when he might return

one year then two then three, day after day, another almanac

he was lost from me

and all that while Edgar implored me to marry, be the mistress of his heart, the mistress of the Grange—Edgar was master by then, his parents had died, Mr. and Mrs. Linton, Mrs. Linton once called Heathcliff *a wicked boy, unfit for a decent house*—while our house festered into a den, the servants fled, the curate stopped calling, Hindley threw himself into gambling while he did his best to die from drink, he told Joseph he was damning his own soul to punish its maker, told Nelly he would cut her throat with the herring-knife and burn us all in our beds, kissed Hareton one moment and shook him senseless the next, though he stayed mainly clear of me, he did not wish to rouse another illness, his wish was that I should marry Edgar—and Edgar implored me, with his blinking dove's eyes

so I married as I had promised, for no true reason any longer except that promise, I married and left the Heights

and Heathcliff returned

on that path in the garden, the path of grief, he returned to me

if I have done wrong, I died for it

Four

The windows have emerged from their ice, the air is milder, she can track the throstles' flight and see the early primrose buds, feel the sweetening year in her own body: what heaven it would be to ride out, now, ride for hours, follow the wind as far as it blows across the moors! But there is nothing she may do, besides follow Ellen about the house—Zillah is gone, and Ellen is here now, summoned from the Grange by Mr. Heathcliff, Ellen said *Mr. Heathcliff says he cannot have you daily in his sight, we must keep out of his way*—but Ellen cannot always be with her, Ellen is busy with her duties of baking and mending and folding and carrying, seeing to the house. So she sits, sighing till she yawns and yawning till she sighs, restless and stalled, Hareton's word, *stalled of doing naught*, her life feels useless.

If she were still at the Grange, she would have Minny, and her dogs, and her little songbirds—although watching the freedom of the birds through these windows has made her think less kindly of a cage—and the whole library to read through, not just the books Ellen has carried over, books Ellen chose, only a few the ones she would have chosen. But if she is truthful to herself, she does not miss the Grange as she once did . . . the maidservants there used to snicker and call her a canary, she did not understand it then but she does now: she was caged. She had known no other place, seen no one besides Papa and Ellen and those servants, not even the curate or a tutor, Papa was her only teacher. When her mother died, Ellen told her, Papa resigned the duties he held as a magistrate, and stopped going into Gimmerton or even to chapel; he made the house and the park her whole world because it was his.

Only once Papa left that world—a journey to faraway London, to visit his sister, her aunt Isabella, who had gone there to live, no one said why; there are no portraits of Aunt Isabella, Ellen says she was a dainty young lady, pale and blue-eyed, like Papa, like Linton—and when Papa had gone, she resolved to go exploring. One of the maids had talked of the fairy-cave and she was wild to see it, she had asked Papa over and over *Now, am I old enough to go to Penistone Crags?* But his answer was always *Not yet, not yet.*

But once he had gone, she galloped Minny away from the garden and the park as if she were flying, across the freedom of the moors to that great bare crag of gritstone rock, to finally glimpse the cave inside—though she did not fully enter there, Hareton warning her off with headshakes and mumbles, Hareton seemed abashed, *Nay, nay, not the kirk!* Hareton knew so much of these hills that she had longed for so long to visit, he told her all about the fairishes, and the goblin-hunter in the marsh, as if he had seen them all, as if he were some wild creature himself, tousled and muddy and strong; it was the first time she saw Hareton, the first day they met.

And her first time too inside this house, EARNSHAW carved over its doors, the pack of watchful, bristling dogs—wolfish Juno took to her straightaway, though Juno was no one's pet—and the little rocking chair by the fire, she hung her hat on the wall and sat at once in that chair as if she had come home. But then Ellen came hurrying to fetch her back, Ellen was in a temper, *If you were aware whose house this is you'd be glad enough to get out! Mr. Linton charged me to keep you in!*

When Papa returned, it was with Linton—Papa cautioning her to treat her cousin gently, *He has lost his mother a very short time since,* would she not understand that without being warned?—Papa meant to enclose Linton too in their quiet little world of park and parlor and library. Yet the next morning Linton was gone: Papa and Ellen said that his father had come for him, and that the journey to visit was much too far for her to travel; Papa and Ellen deceived her. Only Mr. Heathcliff told her truly where Linton lived, though with a bad intent . . . if Linton had stayed at the Grange, lived at the Grange, would he still be alive?

If Linton had lived—she never weeps for him, and cannot miss him or wish him back, he was so peevish and spindling and spiteful, beyond even the trial of his illness; Mr. Heathcliff said once *He's such a cobweb, a pinch would annihilate him,* how strange it feels to agree with Mr. Heathcliff on any topic! Yet it was so. And if Linton had lived, if they were married as others are married, he might have gotten her with child—though he seemed unable, in that way, he was her own age but still seemed half a child himself, wrapped in his robe and sucking sugar-sticks; Hareton is six years older, Hareton is already a man.

Hareton does not speak to her any longer when they pass in the yard or by the gate, or share the kitchen with Ellen of a stormy evening: he only sits staring at the fire, sullen and silent as a brute, grimy from his work in the fields and barn, saying and doing nothing at all until Joseph calls for him, or the shadows send him to bed: how can he be satisfied to exist in such a way! It is true that he tried to teach himself to read, before, or tried to try: but when she overheard him stumbling and drawling and mangling the words—words that he seemed to have chosen especially to annoy her, he chose for his schoolbooks her own books, her own favorite bits of poetry and prose that she loves to repeat aloud—she laughed at him for that, mocked him just as Linton used to mock him, called him *a brute* as Linton called him *a colossal dunce,* and as she mocked and laughed it felt as if she were somehow striking back at Mr. Heathcliff, and at Linton too. Then Hareton gathered up the books and flung them in her lap as if they were bricks, or bones, he shouted at her *Take them, I never want to read them again!* and when she snapped back *I won't have them now, I shall connect them with you, and hate them!* he hurled them into the fire, where she watched them burn . . . why should she ever care if Hareton speaks to her or does not?

So Hareton could never guess what she does now: treading cautious up these stairs when all the house is busy, he and Joseph in the barn, Ellen ironing in the kitchen, Mr. Heathcliff away—she was very careful to watch Mr. Heathcliff ride off toward Gimmerton, if Mr. Heathcliff were to catch her the punishment would be severe: but justice is fully on her side, did not Mr. Heathcliff read all her letters to Linton? Yet she does not seek this room because of Mr. Heathcliff; and she will not stop.

It is her mother she seeks here.

The room is chill and still, not the quiet of emptiness but a silence like a quick breath caught and held. She leaves the door very slightly ajar, keeps her footsteps soft, glances to that door and then the window—once she fled this house by that window, climbing down the fir tree that grows close by the glass as nimbly if she had done it a hundred times before—glances again to the door, then creaks open the oak clothes-press to find inside an old bonnet with discolored ribbons, tries it on, slips it off, examines a pair of stockings splashed with ancient mud, the heels worn nearly through, finds another twist of ribbon, brighter blue, and tucks that into her sleeve. Then she takes up a musty almanac, its days covered in crosses and blotted dots, a mystery, what could that mean or signify?

And then she slides open the box-bed panels, to sit and spell out those names scratched into the paint, **Catherine Linton**

Catherine Heathcliff Catherine Earnshaw, murmuring them like an incantation, like the spells she tells Joseph she casts, before reaching for the books stacked on the ledge, a tiny library smelling of pressed heather and old damp, all marked inside **Catherine Earnshaw, her book,** one has a drawing of Joseph scowling and scolding, and she laughs, then quickly covers her mouth; did her mother draw that?

She pages through each one, reading everything written in the margins—her mother's writing hand is swift, nothing like her own careful script, these words hurry and scrawl together—about Joseph and his awful Scripture lessons, and Nelly, is that Ellen? it sounds like Ellen, and terrible Hindley who was her mother's brother, and made her cry, **I wish my father were back again, Hindley is a detestable substitute,** that means her mother's papa died too, was she there when her papa died?

But the person her mother writes most about is Mr. Heathcliff, page after page, line after line: **H. and I are going to rebel, H. proposes we have a scamper on the moors, H. and I shall go to the Crags at moonrise.** Between those pages are tucked harebells and marsh thistles, a lapwing feather, a papery dead moth, and an envelope of letters, and from that envelope a thick black curl of hair falls straight into her hand, as if someone has placed it there. And these few letters are spotted and splotched as if the ink were rain or tears, **Heathcliff where have you gone? Do you care what I suffer? Cruel Heathcliff, *to leave and* never to think of me!**

Reading these letters makes her feel as if she has been running or riding hard, her breath comes faster, and her mind thrums: her mother was born in this house, grew to be a woman here, yet she lived at the Grange—her old dresses still hang in the wardrobe there, her shoes and boots and silver brushes, all her daily things that Papa kept like secret treasure; Ellen called them relics, *Any relic of the dead is precious if they were valued living*—but how did her mother come to know Papa? to marry Papa? There is nothing of Papa in all this writing, only Mr. Heathcliff . . . Once she and Linton had quarreled fiercely over that, Linton crowing in a kind of triumph *Now I'll tell you something! Your mother hated your father, and she loved mine!*

You little liar! I hate you now!

She did, Catherine, she did, she did!

And she pushed him then, the only moment with Linton that her temper ever rose to fury, she pushed his invalid's chair and at once he collapsed into a racking coughing fit, it went on so long she feared she had killed him, and that ended the dispute—But why had she felt such anger? Did she believe, then, that somehow Linton did *not* lie?

What does she truly know of her mother?

Those empty dresses, that portrait, this room, these letters.

H. and I are going to rebel

Do you care what I suffer?

The door slams.

She drops the letters as she half-scrambles, half-leaps from the bed, ready to run from Mr. Heathcliff—but Mr. Heathcliff is not there, no one is there. Did a breeze gust from the window—no, the lattice is latched, yet the door slammed, was it Ellen? Ellen never comes into this room, has warned her away from it—but still it feels as if someone is near.

She hurries to gather up the letters, and the coarse black curl, and the dead flowers and tokens, hide them back in the books till all appears untouched, all but the dust, her handprints are plain there so she brushes them clean with her skirt's edge, then slips from the room into a sudden hallway chill, the door half-shut behind her.

Downstairs Ellen does not seem even to have heard the

commotion, Ellen sitting busy at her sewing, so she takes a seat beside, to tease and unravel snarls and knotted threads, wondering if she ought to ask the questions she has never asked, means to ask, must ask, why else is she drawn to that room?

Finally she points to the chairs on the hearth, and *When my mother was small,* she says, *that was her seat. You were her nurse, weren't you, Ellen? As you were mine?*

Ellen glances to that chair and sighs, a sharp sigh as if at the memory of a great burden lifted. *She had ways such as I never saw a child take up before. Never so happy as when we were all scolding her at once, and she defying us with her bold, saucy looks.*

Did you love her?

I'll own I did not like her. She put me past my patience fifty times a day.

She winds a coarse black thread around her finger, tightens it, loosens it. *She was—fond of Mr. Heathcliff?*

She was much too fond of Heathcliff, the greatest punishment we could invent was to keep her separate from him. And they both promised fair to grow up as rude as savages! But you need not mind all that, you are not like her at all, my dear young Miss.

Rude and savage, silver brushes, a tombstone buried in heath.

But I'm named for her. When I was born, did she –

When you were born, she was very ill and knew no one, not even Hea—not even your papa. And you were a little moaning doll of a child, it was I who rocked and nursed you from the start. But we should not speak of your mother, she's gone, gone to Heaven I hope, and what's past we must give to God.

She recalls what Joseph said, *right to the devil like your mother before you!* Is her mother gone to Heaven? is she with Papa? Or is she gone, only that, and all she was is present only in that room, in those scrawled pages and unsent letters, and the names scratched into the bed? Cathy, Catherine—the fire suddenly flares, suddenly gutters, then burns evenly again, the sun strikes the windows like a blow. The threads lie tangled in her lap, threaded with black.

Five

Heaven

once we imagined Heaven

it was after Father died, there in his chair as I sang him to sleep, Heathcliff lying with his head in my lap, the wind gasping and roaring in the chimney—he died, and we wept, and Nelly wept, and Joseph scolded us all for crying over a saint in Heaven—and we climbed to the dark of the stairs and clasped hands, we told each other that Heaven must be the most beautiful garden, filled with fields and flowers and every good thing, and Father gone away there to wait for us

I never glimpsed Father beyond the earth, was he not present in that greater dark? or did he not recall me? memory is different here, not like a story held in the mind, more like a brand, or a bruise

I did see Hindley, a quick and groaning fugitive from life—Nelly used to rail at him when he abused Hareton, *Your own flesh and blood! I wonder his mother does not rise from her grave!* his wife Frances dead before him, Hareton's mother dead and watching—does Hindley see Frances, flee Frances? He did not see me, he passed through me like a tremor then was gone, Hindley is his own Hell

and when in my living days I dreamed of Heaven it was not of any garden, none of the sweet glories of earth, but only an empty boundlessness that I wandered like an outcast, in rebellion against a tyrant God who would name this emptiness my home, until the angels in their fleshless anger hurled me back to the dirt, to the heath and the Heights where I opened my eyes again in my own room, joyful tears on my cheeks, a handful of golden crocus on the coverlet, Heathcliff had put them there for me to find

I should have harkened to my dreams

my dreams are true

my life is here

but to find my way back, make my way back, from that emptiness, was first a great and furious bewilderment, then an anguish, a rough journey and a sad heart to travel it! and there, the years are not milestones, time is measured by effort, by the will to hold fast, first, and not to dwindle, to keep intact—otherwise that emptiness would engulf and dispel me, into what those who have never known it call "peace"—and the instant I knew to do so, understood that I could, I turned my face toward home, toward him, making my way as we once crossed the moors without candle or lantern, because we knew where we were bound

I remember my death

that still and sunny afternoon, the parlor, the armchair, the white dress like a shroud around the shattered prison of my body, the world was a mirror yet I could see myself there no longer—and I was so weary! of wanting, and yearning, and tears, it is good to be free of the body when I remember that all-consuming weariness—and the dreariness of meeting death surrounded by those stifling walls, that moist sickroom odor lingering no matter where I lay, a book left on the windowsill as my only companion, while Edgar, even Edgar! took himself outside to enjoy the warm mild air, wander off to the chapel—I thought I would escape from Edgar and from that house, into what I hoped would thrust me beyond and above it all, incomparably so, because life had become unlivable to me, my useless body and my isolated soul and Heathcliff had gone again—taking with him as spoils that imbecile Isabella, no one told me so but I knew—gone where I could not seek him, or any news of him, no one in that house would even mention his name to me

until that afternoon, when Nelly put a paper into my hands, Nelly said *A letter for you, Mrs. Linton*—his answer, finally, to those letters I wrote but could not send!—*Mr. Heathcliff's in the garden, he wishes to see you*

and how my heartbeat, then! fierce as a pounding fist, if I could have opened the door myself I would have, I would have flung it wide, I would have knocked down every wall at the Grange to let him in

but he found his way to me

he found me, and seeing me, he knew

Oh Cathy! oh my life! how can I bear it?

and he smelled of the garden, of grass and heather and life, our life, it was like breath to me! and I breathed him in, I kissed him as he kissed me, sunk my hands into his hair as I used to, as I loved to, I would have held him so until we were both dead

if only I could have

and when I felt his tears on my skin I opened my eyes and saw his pain, it was my pain, I said because it was true *I don't pity you, why shouldn't you suffer? I do*

Wring out my kisses and tears—they'll damn you

You broke my heart, you killed me, will you forget me? How many years do you mean to live after I am gone?

Don't torture me till I'm as mad as yourself, you know I could as soon forget you as my existence! While you're at peace I shall writhe in the torments of hell

I shall not be at peace

but he pulled away from me, he left me, to step behind the armchair, at the fireplace, as my heart thrashed in my body and stifled my breath, a curl I tore from his hair lay in my palm, my hands were already growing colder—*Come here and kneel down again*—but he would not, he hid his face from me—*I only wish us never to be parted! Do come to me*—then finally he did, he held me as if he would keep back the death that I felt already in the room, the edge of his words like the edge of a knife

Teach me now how cruel you've been, Cathy, cruel and false! Nothing could part us, but you of your own will did it—I have not broken your heart, you have, and in breaking it you've broken mine

You left me too, but I forgive you! Forgive me

and we wept together, our tears mingling, tears for every moment of our lives—from the moment I saw him bundled ragged from Father's greatcoat, I spat at him for being nothing I wanted but by the next day I did want him, not as a brother or sweetheart or husband or even as a pleasure, any more than I am always a pleasure to myself, but as Heathcliff, my own being, as I am his—every sorrow, every quarrel, every prank and joy and promise, every minute of the future we might have had, all we were and are, all there in our tears

as Nelly kept watching and warning of Edgar, Edgar, Edgar walking back from the chapel in the ringing of its bells, Edgar opening the gate and entering the house—I had no more business to marry Edgar Linton than I had to be in Heaven!— Nelly fearing that Edgar would blame her for Heathcliff's presence there, fearing that more than she cared that I was dying, she railed at Heathcliff, *Are you going to listen to her ravings? Get up, be quick, hurry down!*

but I held fast to him, I held fast to our life and I cried out with all the strength I still possessed *Oh don't, don't go! it is the last time! Edgar will not hurt us*

Damn the fool! There he is

Heathcliff, I shall die

Hush, hush my darling, I'll stay

and I felt his arms about me more strongly still, his breath as hot and rough and desperate as his kisses, I felt his mouth on mine as if he breathed for me

and then felt nothing, knew nothing, not Edgar's return or what happened to me next, the damp bed, the narrow infant

as the sun set and the moon rose and the sun rose again, and my body cooled in that bed, then in the coffin in the drawing-room, after the maids washed and combed and arranged it, sprinkled scented leaves to mask the smell—already I was past that body, no matter my terror to stay—and Heathcliff kept vigil for me in the garden, he pounded his hands again and again against the brittle ash tree, he gashed his head and wet the bark with his blood, as if he would drive the soul from his body to follow me—he always followed me!—I heard him speak to Nelly as she came to him at last under that tree, I heard his voice like a bell rung in the dark

She's dead, I've not waited for you to learn that

and Nelly wept—Nelly was relieved that I was dead, I knew that, I know all about Nelly now, Nelly our hidden enemy—Nelly wiped her eyes, and said *She recognized nobody from the time you left, she died quietly as a lamb*

did she know how she lied

death was not quiet to me

it was a brutal dwindling, a rushing yet without a sound beyond my slowing blood, my absent breath, I could not move my eyes, I could not move, I watched the spin of the world as I rose and rose above it

and I screamed

I screamed for him

as he groaned at the tree, *Where is she, where is she? not there, not in Heaven, not perished—where? I pray one prayer, I repeat it till my tongue stiffens, may you not rest as long as I am living*

his prayer was true

I did not rest

and my road from that death and that endless heartless peace has been his grief, as mine was his when he rode away from the Heights on the night of the storm, into a different emptiness—when he returned he said to me *I've fought through a bitter life since I last heard your voice*—and that bitterness beat and bled like a living heart between us, it shone like a candle at a garret window when all the world was night, I saw it burn and felt it bleed, it kept me from despair as I drove myself again and again against that distance and that cold, every moment since I left that body

until the moment he wrenched with tears at that snowy lattice beside our bed, and cried out *Come in! Cathy, oh my heart's darling, hear me at last*

and his prayer was answered

by me

for now at last he hears me

and our heaven—ours, not God's nor Nelly's nor Edgar's—our heaven is in sight

Six

In the late morning kitchen, Hareton hunches before the fireplace, head down, hands loose between his knees, unhappy as a hobbled horse: his gun burst while he was out hunting, it drove splinters into his arm and bled him badly before he made his way back, and he is stalled inside until he heals. As she enters, he keeps his stare resolute on the fire, though she says, loud enough to be provoking, *Just like a dog or a cart-horse, isn't he, Ellen? Do you ever dream, Hareton?*

Ellen shakes her head in reproof, sets her knife beside the pile of pared parsnips, wipes her hands. *Mr. Hareton will ask the master to send you upstairs, if you don't behave!*

She shrugs, as if she does not care at all what "the master" may do—master, jailer, uncle, *I shall be your father, all the father you'll have,* Mr. Heathcliff told her that the day he forced her from the Grange to the Heights—though she is as wary of him as the grey cat is of hulking

Thrasher, and for the same reason. But just as the cat will sometimes stare from the mantel to goad Thrasher into barking, she will stare at Mr. Heathcliff when he calls her a worthless bitch, or a damnable jade, daring his anger, swiping back at him *Swear your tongue out, I'll not do anything except what I please!* then leaping, as the cat does, when he raises his hand her way. She has not forgotten the time he did seize and slap her, so hard about the ears it was like being caught in a hailstorm, then thrust her stumbling off as he said *You shall have a daily taste, if I catch such a devil of a temper in your eyes again—I know how to chastise children, you see!* Yet lately when he sees her, he looks away at once, as if he cannot bear even that glimpse of her face.

Now she makes a face at Hareton, a childish thing to do, then steps outside with a slippery handful of parsnip peelings to cross the kitchen yard, where the sudden sun embraces her through the clouds that purl and eddy in the pale blue sky. In the stables, Joseph sorts and grumbles amongst the tack, and glares as she calls to the mare to offer the treat, Joseph interprets her kindly murmurs as a secret hexing, *Harken, she's cursing on 'em!* But she only says *Be off, you tiresome reprobate,* because she has no time now to quarrel; she is thinking, has been thinking, wondering what manner of future hers can be.

As she strokes the mare's soft black nose, she breathes in the warm familiar smells of the stable, rude smells perhaps, animal heat and fresh straw and fresher muck, but she takes pleasure here, as she has come to take pleasure—does she? Yes, growing pleasure in the lift of the wind from the garden gate, and the view from the window of her room, especially on clear nights at moonrise, and the path that winds so steeply down to Gimmerton, like a line traced through the heath; the Grange was lovely, but it is even more beautiful at the Heights. Surely her mother loved it here . . . But was her mother not permitted to visit this house, once she had married Papa? As she herself was not permitted for so long to even know of its existence? Papa detested Mr. Heathcliff, called him diabolical, and indeed no jailer could be more vile: yet when Papa married her mother to keep her always at the Grange, the way he kept her, too, was Papa not a manner of jailer? The idea feels disloyal, but it has the sting of truth.

And as she is, or was, of the Grange, so Hareton is of the Heights, in its brilliant chill and green hardiness, its harshness, Hareton is hard and harsh—and Thrasher barks sharply from the kennel as if sighting an intruder, the mare flicks her ears in alarm—as the sudden memory rises, a memory of Hareton fetching a fine wriggling terrier pup from that kennel, to put into her hands and ease her tears, tears she shed at learning that he was her cousin, Hareton in his grimy waistcoat and muddied boots, *he's not my cousin, my cousin is a gentleman's son!* When that gentleman was Mr. Heathcliff! And she had not yet laid eyes on Linton! What a foolish thing for her to have thought, and said . . . Hareton belongs here as Linton never did or ever could, Hareton loves to ride and roam as she would love to ride and roam. What if she had been let to visit here, as a child? would she and Hareton have grown, then, to be friends? out on the hills, among the fairishes, playing and riding, hardy and free—

    —as the mare lays back her ears and stamps a hoof in alarm, and *Wisht, wisht!* she murmurs, looking to see who has spooked her so—Joseph has gone, and Hareton is in the house, Ellen is in the house, Mr. Heathcliff is away, who could it be? for now she feels a presence too, a strangeness like darkness in midday—and see, the red blanket from the bench has been pushed onto the floor, as if by a passing hand, whose hand? Slowly she steps from the stall to the doorway, as if she walks on sudden ice, stands in the breathing breeze—

    —as another memory rises, of Papa's dying smile, *I am going to her,* going where? Where is her mother? In the flowery grave in the churchyard? Or in the room upstairs? She opens her mouth to speak, to say as Mr. Heathcliff did on the night he wept, *Come in, come in*— but what will happen if she calls out now? Who will answer?

Come in—

—the words in her mind if not on her lips, her heart beats in her throat like a second voice, Thrasher lets out one strangled startled yelp—

Come in, come in!

—but even as she starts to speaks the strangeness ceases, the doorway stands empty, the yard is empty, the mare whickers mildly in her stall. Thrasher salutes with a bark as she crosses that yard, beneath the sun swept by silver-edged clouds, her hands tucked beneath her arms for warmth, she is suddenly chilled, the air is so cold—

—in the shadow of the Heights, its dark roof and walls and gates a fortress line against the vastness of the sky and the heath, how long shall she bide here? As long as Mr. Heathcliff pleases? Nothing pleases Mr. Heathcliff, though he seems, these days, to take less notice of them all, he is in and out of the house at odd hours, and barely speaks to them when he is present; he seems, like the mare and like Thrasher, to be drawn and distracted, disturbed, by what is not there.

What does Mr. Heathcliff see?

And will Mr. Heathcliff send her out of his sight for good, send her back to the Grange? No, even though that house will be empty, since its silly jabbering tenant, Mr. Lockwood, will not bide there again, Ellen says. The night Mr. Lockwood was driven in fright from her mother's room, why was he so frightened? She ought to have asked, but all she said when he spoke to her was *Take the road you came;* and soon Mr. Lockwood will take that road, back to London, Ellen says.

Ellen has told her more than once what a kind gentleman Mr. Lockwood is; kind? Can Ellen mean his sole courtesy in carrying over to her *A letter from your old acquaintance, the housekeeper*—Ellen was still at the Grange then, she saw Mr. Lockwood daily—*Ellen Dean never wearies of talking about you!* Mr. Lockwood dropped that letter in her lap like a bird drops a berry, but her own *What is that?* alerted Hareton: Hareton seized that letter, not to read it—he cannot read—but to give to Mr. Heathcliff. But then, because she cried, Hareton gave it back to her—he threw it, but he gave it—Hareton marks her tears, he has tried to mend them—

—as the thought comes like a murmur in her ear, of what her life here might be, or become, if she and Hareton could in some way be friends, he is her kin after all, her cousin, kin to her mother too—

—and now the rising sound of hoofbeats, she turns to see Mr. Heathcliff riding up the path from Gimmerton, riding hard and almost recklessly, driving his horse as if he is pursued by, or pursuing, some terrible goal—what *is* his goal? Other than to punish and stifle, keep her prisoner until he is as old and bent by his hate as Joseph? Mr. Heathcliff was as young as Hareton once—and her mother must once have stood in just this spot, to watch him ride in, go and meet him at the stables—

—but to entirely avoid meeting him, she hurries back inside, past the pigeons' sudden flutter in their cote, into the kitchen where Hareton still has not moved from the fire. She means to continue through and up to her room, but an impulse stops her, a flush not of warmth but cold and *I know why Hareton never speaks*, she says, standing where Hareton cannot help but see her, *when I am in the kitchen*, purportedly to Ellen busy thumping a heavy twist of dough. *What do you think, Ellen—he began to teach himself to read, and because I laughed, he burned his books. Was he not foolish?*

Hareton's face goes dark with temper, or is it shame? as Ellen shakes her head: *Were you not naughty, Miss? Answer me that.*

The changeable sun finds the windows again, its shine briefly rivaling the fire's light, making Hareton turn his head in a sudden squint, then turn away again, rapid and awkward, so that he will not, cannot, meet her eyes; it is the way Mr. Heathcliff avoids the sight of her, yet not that way at all—so *Perhaps I was*, she says, and as she says it means it: kin to him, friend to him, it was wrong to do as she did to him, slam shut the door of his mind, how might she make amends? *Hareton, if I gave you a book, would you take it now? I'll try!*

She reaches for the volume on the windowsill, a lively tome of Greek and Roman tales, myths of flying horses and talking trees, heroes and gods—Joseph has called it a foul heathen's primer, another reason to prize it—and leans to place that book, balance it, carefully on Hareton's knee. At once he flings it off, but to the floor not the fire, he mutters *Give over!* while looking, still, as far from her as he can. So *I shall put it here*, she says, keeping her tone careful and inviting, *here in the table drawer, and I'm going up*—murmuring to Ellen *Watch whether he touches it!* as she quickly quits the room, she is almost smiling—

—but her smile dies at the foot of the stairway, in the sudden silent presence of Mr. Heathcliff, standing still as carven whinstone, staring up to where nothing stands, only shadows. Approaching quiet as a careful cat, she means to pass without a word, provoke from him no attention or rebuke—

—yet *Catherine Linton*, he says, one hard hand on her arm to halt her, half-turning from his contemplation of those shadows to examine her, as if she is a picture, a portrait, an apparition, his hand too is very cold. *Catherine Linton, you look less a Linton than did my sniveling son. All the Lintons are sniveling and soft, Edgar and Isabella would wither at the first cross. But you're no weakling.*

She stares back, half in wariness, half defiance—she had cursed him before, under that portrait of her mother, *Nobody loves you! nobody will cry for you when you die!* does he remember that?—but for once Mr. Heathcliff does not seem angry: his face is somber, his eyes are troubled, his whole aspect is troubled, what does he want with her? She should not speak, but—*You used to visit there,* she says. *At the Grange.*

I did. Once or twice too often.

You married Aunt Isabella, Linton's mother, you said once that you and my papa quarreled for it. You said that he wronged you—

Edgar Linton—his stare changing as he drops his grip, he looks at her now the way he looked when he broke her little golden locket, to take for himself the side that held her mother's tiny portrait, and crush the other, of Papa, to splinters with his foot—*Edgar Linton's whole existence was a wrong to me. And his happiest days were over when your days began. Get upstairs, witch, and out of my sight.*

Seven

the Lintons always called me dear Miss Earnshaw

the Lintons fully believed that they bettered me by their flatteries and comforts, petit-point and spinet lessons, ringlets and a beaver hat—after their bulldog chewed me bloody for a thief!—but it was not so, never so, it was like a stone in my shoe when I tried to be that young lady of the Grange, stroll with Isabella, dance with Edgar, curb my temper and my tongue, stay inside when the wind was rising or the night was breathing at the windows, make believe I did not know life as I did, its horrors and its bliss

to be a Linton should be no one's ambition

the Lintons believed too that Heathcliff was unworthy of their notice, that he was a ploughboy, a bastard, worse than a brute

until Isabella took her lunatic's fancy to him

Isabella! it was laughable, worse than laughable, as deplorable as if a coddled canary sought to mate with a hunting goshawk—when I saw what she was about, I gave her the truth of what she was, and what Heathcliff was, I told her that Heathcliff could never love a Linton, that he would crush her like a sparrow's egg—but she would not believe me and she would not desist, she said *You're a dog in the manger, Cathy! I love Heathcliff more than you ever loved Edgar, and he might love me if you would let him!*

so to punish her for her impertinence, and put a final end to the business, I put her together with Heathcliff in the parlor, and told her ridiculous secret—*I'm proud to show you someone who dotes on you more than myself, I expect you to feel flattered! My poor little sister-in-law is breaking her heart over your physical and moral beauty*—as if Isabella should ever taste either! Isabella with her yellow curls and petty tears, her vixen's temper, she scratched me with her sharp little nails to escape that parlor scene, I told her to begone, I told Heathcliff he must not notice her further

but her spoiled greed to have what was only mine spurred his own greed for what could not, could never, satisfy him, and aided his belief in its imagined power—to own the Grange! to own the Heights! as if mere property could repair our damage, or restore the years that were lost—he was sick with it already, that greed and vengeance, rotten seeds planted by Hindley

and I feared it for him, for did I not once believe the same? that to be Mrs. Linton would somehow save us both?

I was right to fear

more years lost to the cold

for when Nelly caught him courting Isabella on the sly, he was fully unrepentant, he stood there in the kitchen of the Grange and told me that I had treated him infernally, had leveled our palace and given him a hovel for a home, that I was a fool if I thought he would suffer unrevenged—he said, purely to wound me, *I have a right to kiss her if she chooses, I'm not your husband*

If you like Isabella you shall marry her

If I imagined you really wished me to marry her I'd cut my throat

I won't repeat my offer of a wife—quarrel with Edgar, deceive his sister, you'll revenge yourself on me

yet even then I might have diverted him and kept him from that hell, kept myself from the hell of waiting—revenge takes time—but no, Nelly must stir the brew, oh, we'll make her rue! Nelly using Edgar for her stirring-stick, rousing up all his old disgust and dread of Heathcliff, till Edgar accosted us right there in the kitchen with his wide eyes and pale cheeks, his rebukes of our moral poison, Edgar called me disgraceful and improper for keeping Heathcliff as my friend, told Heathcliff he was barred from ever visiting the Grange, *Sir I require your instant departure!*

so I locked us all in together, I threw the key into the fire

Make an apology, Edgar, or be beaten—I wish Heathcliff may flog you sick, for daring to think an evil thought of me

Cathy, this lamb of yours threatens like a bull, it is in danger of splitting its skull against my knuckles

and Edgar looked just as he had when we were children, at that awful Christmas fête, when Heathcliff flung hot applesauce in his face and he sobbed into his pocket handkerchief—the master of the Grange! quivering like a mouse in a hole, even when he tried to knock Heathcliff down he failed—I would have felt shame for Edgar if he had any for himself, but as a Linton he believed himself always correct, always justified in whatever he did or meant to do, to anyone, to me

so he summoned the menservants with pistols and bludgeons, as if to slay a monster, and Heathcliff smashed the lock with a poker and left

left me with my nerves at such a pitch that I felt as if I might do anything, grind my teeth until my mouth bled, stiffen like a corpse, starve my body to faltering, in that mounting certainty of loss and sundering, our sundering again, knowing Heathcliff would find a way to take Isabella and feed his sickness, and punish me, punish us both

and he did

as I lay for days ice-locked in that bedchamber, until finally Edgar came—ever found when least wanted! that was Edgar—to stand by my bed in his bloodless dismay, *Am I nothing to you anymore? Do you love that wretch?* but I could not bear to hear Heathcliff's name from Edgar's mouth ever again, I said that I would spring from the window first, make a final end that way

and this time the fever tormented me differently, it showed me like a dream my life as the lady of Thrushcross Grange, as Catherine Linton, an exile, an outcast, as if I had been thrust out of my true self in one great grieving stroke—separated by Hindley from the bed I shared with Heathcliff, separated by marriage from the life I should have lived—while I burned and begged for traitor Nelly to unfasten the window, so I could at least breathe the air off the moors as I used to, be a girl again, Cathy Earnshaw, half-savage, hardy and free

I chose freedom at least in my burying-spot, not under the chapel roof among those waxy Lintons, but out in the open air

yet the Grange remained my living tomb

while Heathcliff made Isabella his false bride

after my death she taunted him, *If I were you I'd go stretch yourself over her grave and die like a faithful dog, the world is surely not worth living in now, is it?*—that was the love she had for him

Isabella! covetous sister, the worst of all the Lintons—as a girl she called Heathcliff a *Frightful thing! Put him in the cellar, papa!* to Mr. Linton who thought Heathcliff and I were young villains come to steal his rent-day receipts, when truly we had come on that sad dark rainy Sunday to peep in the long windows of the Grange and see what looked to us like perfect comfort—warmth, and quiet, no one shouting, no one reaching for the whip—then laugh at those two milky brats as they pouted over nothing, we made groanings and growls to terrify them

we did terrify them

I never saw Isabella again, not in life or ever after—perhaps she is reunited with her brother, their flimsy spirits smothered in peace, spoiled children who believed the world must have been made for them, all Lintons are soft

but now there is another Catherine Linton

she is called Catherine Heathcliff—from wedding Isabella's meager son, another of Heathcliff's errors—and is as fair as Edgar, with yellow curls like Isabella's,

but her eyes are mine

she came from me, she is the infant they took from me, a child whose existence I could barely credit, a living thing come from that dying body

I did not see her, I could not see her truly till she came to the Heights—Edgar kept her from it every way he could, kept her where she would know nothing beyond the Grange, not the moors, not the Crags, not even Gimmerton, he would have covered up the sky if he could—Edgar meant for her to know nothing of me, be nothing like me

but I see her now

she is the age I was when I married Edgar

and she is not afraid of me

as Edgar was afraid, Edgar would not care to know how it was for me after he closed my sightless eyes with his pious prayers, how I fared in that other, greater exile, that bleakness like ten thousand times ten thousand nights—Edgar would never pray, as Heathcliff did, for me to haunt him, Edgar was afraid of me when I was alive!

but she is not afraid

though she has felt my cold, she senses my presence, my essence, hears my whispers, my urgings for her to know Hareton

I come closer, very close

and I feel her curiosity burning like a lamp, her warm need to know more of me, I see her look for me at the window, in the stables, in my room—she dares to go there, rummage through my things, she tried to wear my old church bonnet! did Nelly never show her those dresses at the Grange? Edgar never had, Edgar kept them as dead relics—and in the box bed with the books, my books and hers

and she says *Come in*

like Heathcliff

she and Heathcliff together, their pain and their belief, their human hearts, have welcomed me back from the cold

though Heathcliff loathes her still for the manner of her birth, for being Edgar's child—when he fathered a child on Isabella!—but he must learn better, learn who she is

she is my daughter

Catherine Linton, Catherine Heathcliff, Catherine Earnshaw, another Catherine has come home to the Heights

Eight

To her great surprise and greater disappointment, Hareton did not touch the book of myths, it lay still in the drawer the next morning; was the lure of the words not strong enough? her invitation not frank enough? Next she tried reading it aloud, ostensibly to Ellen, stopping once, then again, then again, at exciting precipice moments, leaving the book where he must find and take it up; yet he has not taken it; he ignores her still. He has even begun to smoke a pipe as Joseph does, two dour figures on either side of the fire, puffing and glowering; it is disheartening, maddening, to see Hareton act so, she must rouse him from it, but how shall she do that?

Finally Joseph takes himself shuffling from the house, to drive some cattle to Gimmerton—may they trample him and free themselves!—and Mr. Heathcliff is gone off again; no one knows where he goes, sometimes riding, sometimes on foot, sometimes

coming back long after dark, Ellen says that Mr. Heathcliff will soon
be unwell if he continues his roving.

At this moment Ellen is busy ironing, patting and tweaking the
fresh linen—Ellen is so house-proud about those linens, and the
copper pots and polished clock and shine of the floor, as if Ellen feels
herself to be the mistress here—Ellen is too busy to take any notice
of her, as she crosses to where Hareton sits in the chimney corner,
smoking like a chimney again: she places herself where he cannot
avoid her, to say what she has determined to say, the bold and simple
truth, a truth as much for herself as for him—

*I've found out, Hareton, that I want—that I'm glad—that I would like you
to be my cousin now.*

His answer is a growl, he will not look at her.

Hareton, do you hear?

Go to the devil, and let me be!

No, I won't! You shall take notice of me, you're my cousin —

I shall have naught to do with you—side out, this minute!

As she turns back, balked, to the window seat, she feels hot tears
rise, of frustration and of something else, something deeper—hurt,
she did not expect that Hareton could hurt her, but he has; she cares

if Hareton cares for her—

—and Ellen must be watching after all, because she calls out from beside her ironing pile, *Mr. Hareton, your cousin repents, you should be friends. Companions*—

A companion! When she hates me? Not if it made me a king!

Now her tears overspill, she sobs outright: *It's not I who hate you, it's you who hate me! As much as Mr. Heathcliff does*—

You're a damned liar—why have I made him angry then, by taking your part a hundred times? And that when you sneered at me—

I didn't know you took my part!

Go on plaguing me, and I'll step in yonder and say you worried me out of the kitchen—

I was miserable and bitter at everybody, wiping her tears as a child might, with her hand across her eyes. *But now I thank you,* stepping back before him, *and I beg you to forgive me,* reaching out to him, her hand wet with those tears, *what else can I do besides?*

Yet his hands are still clenched, he will not look up, there in his grubby waistcoat spotted with train-oil, his dark tangled hair, his arm still bound from the bleeding, Hareton this close smells of wood smoke and pipe smoke and another scent she cannot name, she wants him as her friend, she wants him—so she bends to him, her hair falling forward to enclose them both, she kisses his raspy cheek—

—and that kiss sends a thrill through her mind as well as her body, as if she has done exactly the thing she must do—

—though Ellen, watching, shakes her head, Ellen does not approve, she feels the blush rising but knows she has done no wrong, she murmurs to Ellen *I must show him some way that I like him, that I want to be friends.* And while Hareton sits dumbfounded in the silence of that kiss, as if he has been shaken, thrust, into some other place entirely, she hurries to wrap the book of myths in clean white paper, and tie it with the fine twist of blue ribbon she found in her mother's room, addressing it in plain writing to MR HARETON EARNSHAW, saying to Ellen *Tell him, if he'll take it, I'll come and teach him to read it right, and if he refuses, I'll go upstairs and never tease him again.*

She perches on a chair behind the table, as Ellen does as she is bid—Hareton will not take the book in hand, so Ellen places it on his knee; this time he does not knock it to the floor, and then she sits, her forehead resting on her hands, waiting in steep suspense for the rustling of the wrapping, that sound will mean her life has changed—

—and when it comes, she follows it at once, to sit close beside Hareton, and *Say you forgive me,* softly, so only he can hear. *You can make me so happy by speaking that little word.*

His answer in return is not a word, yet fully eloquent; his hands are unclenched now, they tremble.

And you'll be my friend?

Nay, you'll be ashamed of me every day of your life, and I cannot bide it—

So you won't be my friend?

He looks to her finally, half a look, and she smiles: he smiles too, half a smile; she opens the book.

And together they turn the pages, his hand on the book, her hand on his shoulder: all the fine bright illustrations, and the words that she shows him he knows, some of them, already, she will open this world to him as he opened the moors to her. Time passes in the daily world of the kitchen, minutes and minutes, an hour, more, but they are elsewhere, wandering together—

—until Joseph returns, silenced for once, so utterly aghast to find them sitting so close together. Counting out onto his opened Bible the money he gathered in Gimmerton, Joseph uses those bank-notes as a way to pry Hareton from her side: *Take these in to the master, lad, and bide with him. We must side out, this room's not seemly nor proper—*

Come, Catherine, Ellen says, *I've done my ironing, we must 'side out' too.*

Hareton, rising, as unwilling to leave him as he is to see her go, their smile shared, his dark eyes so much like her own, like her mother's, *I'll leave this on the chimney-piece, and tomorrow we'll read another.*

Any books ye leave, Joseph threatens, *ye shall be lucky to find again—*

Your library, her pointed nod at his thick black Bible, still lying open on the table, *shall pay for ours*—still smiling, she means it and Joseph knows she means it; their picture book will not be harmed.

Climbing the stairs, humming a song the maids at the Grange used to sing, *As I came thru' the north, merrie company I sought,* does Hareton like to sing? As she readies for bed, the moon enters her window like a benediction, and she kneels in its light, not in prayer, but in that continuing feeling of rightness, the feeling that she has finally found the sweeter way to live, she and Hareton together.

The next morning, before breakfast, they pace out a new flower garden, she pondering which plants they shall fetch over from the Grange, as he clears away the black currant and gooseberry bushes to make the ground ready. But when Ellen sees their handiwork, she scolds at once, alarmed and hissing *Joseph's currants! That will be shown to the master, there will be a fine explosion—Mr. Hareton, you made that mess at her bidding?*

I'll tell him, Hareton says, looking at her, *that I did it.*

And before they gather for the meal, Ellen is scolding again—*Don't talk to your cousin too much, Mr. Heathcliff will be mad at you both*—but she only shrugs; she has a handful of primroses hidden in her skirt, and one by one she sticks them into Hareton's plate of porridge, to make him smile, to make another garden, to show him that, together, they need not care for anyone's permission or denial, not even Mr. Heathcliff's—

—sitting there at the head of the table, she looks to see if he is watching—but sees instead Mr. Heathcliff's face so fully preoccupied, so openly pained, that she pauses, regarding him for once not as her cruel tormentor, or Hareton's oppressor, but as Mr. Heathcliff who once was Heathcliff, as her mother once was Cathy, **H. and I are going to rebel** . . . does he feel, as she does, that strange insistent presence? does he feel the cold, has he felt it all these years?

Then Hareton darts a glance her way, covert and sweet, and she sticks another primrose in his plate, this time he cannot help but give a little smothered laugh—

—and Mr. Heathcliff startles, as if surprised to find himself there at the table amongst them, his glare is aimed immediately at her: *Don't remind me of your existence! I thought I had cured you of laughing.*

Hareton mutters, *It was me.*

What do you say?

Hareton stares down at his plate; she bites her lip, Ellen pours more tea. The table is silent again, stays silent, the meal is almost safely through—

—when Joseph appears at the door, his face in furrows like a child's about to cry, mumbling in a rage about taking his wages and leaving service, *It fair busts my heart!* until Mr. Heathcliff interrupts: *Cut it short! Is the fool drunk? Hareton, is it you he's finding fault with?*

I've pulled up two or three bushes, but I'm going to set 'em again.

Why have you pulled them up?

Before Hareton can speak again, she does. *To plant flowers—I'm the only person to blame, I wished him to do it.*

Mr. Heathcliff is startled anew, startled by her, she can see that. *And who the devil gave you leave to touch a stick about the place?*

You shouldn't grudge a few yards of earth, when you've taken all my land—

Your land! You never had any—

And Hareton's too, giving him back glare for glare, biting the crust of her breakfast bread: her fear is less now than her anger, this is her house, hers and Hareton's. *Hareton and I are friends now—I shall tell him all about you, he'll not obey you anymore.*

Mr. Heathcliff looks suddenly confounded, as if he does not for once know how to respond, until his rage boils anew, he raises a hand: *Dare you rouse him against me?*

If you strike me, Hareton will strike you—

If Hareton does not turn you out of this room—drag her off! Do you hear?

—and Mr. Heathcliff is out of his chair, Hareton is out of his chair, Hareton imploring her *Have done!* But now Mr. Heathcliff's hard hand is in her hair, a twisting, intolerable pain, she stifles a cry while Hareton tries to free her, entreating Mr. Heathcliff not to hurt her, Mr. Heathcliff seems ready to tear her to scraps—

—but then the pressure eases, the pain stops, his hand drops from her head to her arm, he holds her as he had by the stairs, staring as intently into her face, then *Go with Mrs. Dean,* he says, his eyes are glittering, can it be tears again? *And if I see Hareton listen to you, I'll send him seeking his bread where he can get it. Your love will make him an outcast, and a beggar—Nelly, take her! All of you, leave!*

She hurries out and swiftly up the stairs, safe in her room to stay as safely absent through dinner, Ellen will carry her a plate. But when dinnertime comes, Mr. Heathcliff sends for her to come down, though he does not look at her, or speak to anyone at the table; he barely eats, then is gone again, on foot, on another of his secret errands. Watching him hurry toward the garden gate, Ellen shakes her head, mystified: *We shall have a fit of illness. I cannot conceive what he is doing!*

And she and Hareton exit too, outside again to the little patch of dirt: Hareton begins to replant the wilting currant bushes, pointing out to her another space, *I'll dig there*—beside the fir trees, at the end of the house—*and shift our garden.*

We shouldn't have to shift. This land is yours as much as mine.

Wisht, have done—

If it were not for Mr. Heathcliff's wickedness—

If he were the devil, no matter, I'd stand by him—

He has been wicked to us both! He hated your father, he hated mine—

If I spoke ill of your father, you wouldn't have it. Speak ill of me instead, as you used to, with such a sad and steadfast frown that after a moment she shakes her head, not in negation but agreement, she helps him right the bushes, pile the fresh dirt, while the sun warms them both. All the father you'll have, that is Mr. Heathcliff to Hareton, and she will not wound him further by trying to put right what he cannot see as wrong; she will not pit him against Mr. Heathcliff again.

Their harmony restored, this afternoon's reading lesson is even more absorbing, the book shared between their laps, teacher and pupil close together on the settle, Hareton diligent, she determined: Hareton is quick, how could she ever have thought him otherwise? She will teach him everything she knows. Ellen sits nearby with her mending, the fire gives them all its calm heat, the day slowly winds into evening—

—and suddenly Mr. Heathcliff is at the door, his face without expression, staring in at them all like a traveler lost in the dusk. She feels herself brace for whatever is coming, feels Hareton beside her bracing too, as Mr. Heathcliff crosses to stand over them, takes the book from Hareton's hand—

—but then hands it back without a word, gesturing without anger for her to quit the room; she does at once, Hareton does just after— yet she can hear Mr. Heathcliff halt Ellen by saying, *A poor conclusion, is it not?* his voice also without anger, she has never heard Mr. Heathcliff speak this way before. *Everything is ready and in my power, my old enemies have not beaten me, I could do it*—Do what? Ready for what? and she lingers, unseen and listening, trying to puzzle out what he may mean, what may be her future, hers and Hareton's. *But where is the use? Nelly, there is a strange change approaching, I'm in its shadow*—*Those two who have left the room, I earnestly wish she were invisible. He moves me differently*—*I can give them no attention, anymore.*

And Ellen too sounds puzzled: *But what do you mean by a change, Mr. Heathcliff?*

I shall not know that, till it comes—

You have no feeling of illness, you are not afraid of death?

Afraid? No!

—as from the outer doorway she hears a whistle, softer than a pigeon's coo, once then twice: Hareton whistling to draw her attention, Hareton beckoning her outside to the darkness of the yard—

—under the cooling sky suspended in the last moments between sunset and starlight, as the eddying wind ruffles Hareton's heavy brown locks, as together they enter the deeper and welcoming dark of the stable, the horses' nickers and slow whuffing sighs—their stable, their horses, their evening, their world—and the red blanket slowly drops to the floor, as if tugged by the wind or by a reaching hand, so she reaches for it, settles it upon the bench, and Hareton takes his seat at her side.

Nine

Heathcliff

Heathcliff you have aged, you have lived in time—though your hair is still thick and black, your step still quick—you have aged

but not changed

yet still you thrash in those throes of your own making, that attenuated, grasping vengeance, the master of two great houses and of nothing at all

I feel his misery—his miseries have always been my miseries—as he feels the cold around me, gripping all the closer as I press closer to him, reach for him as he yearns for me—but the massive cold of those black crags, of death itself, is still less than the cold of our separation

all our separations

our life together begun like a parting eased—though at first I could not understand his Liverpool chatter, nor he mine, still we knew each other—Hindley hated him all the more for it, Hindley swore that Heathcliff had broken the little fiddle on purpose, *Father carried home that fiddle for me! Father said he wished to hear music!* blubbering on and on until I laughed, *You can't play the fiddle, Hindley!* but when Hindley raised his hand to strike me, Heathcliff struck first and bloodied his nose, and Hindley cursed us, threw clods of muck at us as we ran off

to the moors, where I taught Heathcliff all I knew, how to mount and ride a pony, find the lapwings' nests and build feather castles, taught him later everything the curate taught me, shared my books to keep him from falling back into ignorance, and rebel against Hindley that way too—though he did fall, deeper and deeper, into that degradation, the same that he inflicts on Hareton! as I fell into the flattery and folly of the Lintons

and after our strained reunion, past my convalescence at the Grange, the fine lady come home in her silks and beaver hat, he began to pull away from my caresses, to doubt our love—later he confessed to Nelly he had done so, *I was a fool to fancy for a moment that she valued Edgar Linton's attachment more than mine, Cathy has a heart as deep as I have, how can she love in him what he has not?*—though never did I doubt him, Edgar could not have loved me as much in eighty years as Heathcliff did every day

so to mend his doubt and his distance, I told him we must go to the fairy-kirk, go inside, together

the maids said *At the fairy-kirk, you'll see the odd 'uns marry!*—the odd ones, the fairishes who made the ancient rule that when a loving couple enter and pledge there, they are truly wed—but if a year passes and they do not marry in the outer world, they must haunt the rock forever, or if either should choose to marry another, that one shall die

and together in that clefted rock we gave ourselves, all of ourselves, the taste of our kisses and the sweat of our bare strong bodies, pressed together in the trickle and glow, how his hands shook! and I gasped and laughed in our pleasure, our happiness shone like a moon in that stony dark, Heathcliff said *I'm your husband, no one can ever part us now*

oh my bonny love

the maids had shown me how to use the pennyroyal and the yarrow, to make certain no child would come from our coupling—a child makes a future, and what future had we, under Hindley's rule? we could not even house ourselves! though Heathcliff said as we walked back beneath that lovers' moon, *We shall live together at the Heights, I promise you*

How? with Hindley swearing every day to send you back where you came from?

Nelly told me once that I was a kidnapped prince in disguise, from China, or India

Shall we go there then

Don't mock—we shall live at the Heights, Cathy, you'll see

but in a few months he had gone, gone off—he never said how or where he went, those years, did he go to China, to India—and I was left waiting

for our next reunion, in the garden at the Grange, it was like a dream to see him standing in that mellow sunset gloom, in a gentleman's fine black waistcoat, his hair trimmed back, but still Heathcliff, always Heathcliff—I felt that I could breathe again, that life had come alive again, I felt my heart leap like a beast upon him as I gathered him to me, *I shall not be able to believe that I've seen, and touched, and spoken to you once more!* and he gathered me, he said *You'll not drive me off again*

but he parted us himself, then, with his sickness, with Isabella

and then came back to me, as I lay in that anteroom of death, the sunny window armchair, still waiting, waiting

then back again to my raw new grave, in the punishing snow and sleet—no one else was there that night, Edgar made sure to kept his grief indoors, and dry—through the twin howls of the doubled cold I heard Heathcliff crying, crying out, *I'll have her in my arms again!* as he snatched a spade from the tool-house, to dig without stopping, flinging snow and mud and peat as if he would strip the earth from me, tear it to pieces, he scraped the new wood of my coffin, he would have cracked the lid in two and pulled free my limp body, pressed it close to his own, *If I can only get this off, I wish they may shovel the earth in over us both!*

but that was not the way, not the fairy-kirk but the churchyard, so I stopped him, I drew near as I could through eternity's distance— and he felt me as a breath, a sigh, I knew he felt me and he knew that I was with him, not in that box but there beside him

and we might have gone on together that very night, in that rush of consolation and unspeakable relief—he cloaked my body again in peat and coffin wood, I urged him home, and all that way he spoke to me, *I shall see you, I know I shall see you at the Heights!*—and there would be no more parting, ever, I blessed the tears freezing on his cheeks, my hope burned like a branch crackling in ice

but at the doorstep hate detained him, he fought with Hindley, and wrangled with Isabella—neither of them worth a single breath he ever drew—no matter that I struggled to keep near him, near the earth he trod, while that emptiness sought so voraciously to claim me, devour me beyond any pain or love

just as I had seen in my dream

the dream Nelly would not let me speak of, she feared it as a premonition, a glimpse of real catastrophe, in that at least Nelly spoke truth—for in that dream I journeyed to the fairy-kirk to be wed, in a pale gown beaded with drops of dew like unshed tears, it snagged on thistles and red thorns, dragged sodden through the beck, the harebell crown fell from my hair as I journeyed there alone

all alone

and when I ventured into that bleak embrace of stone, I knew at once I had done wrong to be there, I turned to go back—but there was no way back, the moors had vanished, there was nothing outside but that waiting emptiness and unknowable cold—and I screamed, I screamed without air or sound, I screamed myself awake, opening my eyes upon the day that Heathcliff would leave me, and Edgar would ask me to wed

and in this emptiness there is no weariness, but it is a constant struggle—Heathcliff has called it a long fight, but has prolonged it almost past all bearing, he told Nelly it was *a strange way of killing, not by inches, but by hairsbreadths, night and day, incessantly, remorselessly*—his doing! not mine!

though he has done my work as well, to bring my daughter home

and he learns, because I work to show him, that she is mine, Catherine who meets his aching rage with her growing strength, and Hareton now beside her—Hareton is as strong as she, how little Hareton resembles Hindley!—they will shift him at last from his fixation on punishment and property, demonstrate to him how useless were all his labors—Catherine is leagued with me to do so, ever since that night the stranger came

the night Heathcliff truly heard me, his whisper, *Is anyone there?*

now he hears me daily

on the stairs

in the stable

on his long circling walks on the moors

on the path to Gimmerton, riding with all his might

lying abed but not asleep

hears me whisper and call even as he rails at Catherine and shouts at Hareton, gives orders to malignant Joseph, speaks to Nelly who listens while understanding nothing—Nelly marks how haggard his body grows, she asks him again and again if he feels ill, Nelly believes he shall fall ill or go mad, she fears what may happen if he dies

she has feared so ever since that day at the Grange when he told her what he did when Edgar died, how he bribed the sexton, busy digging Edgar's grave, to free my coffin, so he might open it and see that body's face once more, its clothing already gone to rags—the peat preserves, but the air brings rot, the sexton warned him of that, the sexton was afraid of him, too afraid not to do as he asked!—so he contented himself with striking loose one side of that coffin, to be pulled away when his body is buried there, so our dust might mingle—Nelly was blanched and shocked to hear it, she called him wicked, she said he had disturbed the dead

I laughed

and he said *I disturbed nobody, Nelly, and you'll have a better chance of keeping me underground when I get there*

underground! as if it matters what that vacant flesh will do, or not do, or become, in time's hands or any other's, as if we shall care for that! when the distance between us has been conquered we shall be where we should always have been, where he promised me we would be

at the Heights

and we will have all that eternity is when all parting is over, a communion and commingling such as our love in the fairy-kirk was only the merest taste, our souls shall have bliss no living body could withstand

we shall be utterly together

Heathcliff

oh see him look, and stare—see the sweat shine on his forehead— he told Nelly *I ought to have sweat blood—she showed herself, as she was in life, a devil to me! I've been the sport of torture*

who tortured who, my bonny love

Heathcliff

if I dare you, will you venture? we've dared far worse—it asks so little, to cross, finally, to me

if you do, I'll keep you

Heathcliff

as I died in that chair, he said to me, *Do I want to live?*

do come to me, Heathcliff

Ten

Down by the morning gate, on her knees in the tufting grass, she is so busy gathering up primrose roots—Hareton is planting their garden border—that she does not even hear Mr. Heathcliff approach until he is almost upon her, his breathing loud and ragged, his coat torn at the sleeve, is that mud on his face? and is Mr. Heathcliff smiling? Mr. Heathcliff gives her barely a glance as he passes, he says *Begone now, fast as you can*—

—so she runs to outpace him, back to the fir trees, to Hareton, and Ellen—Ellen is with them often, as watchful as a nursemaid—Hareton told her after breakfast, when Mr. Heathcliff did not come to the table, *He quit the house again, last night late. Nelly says he told her he's got a rare wish, but nowt else about it.* And when she asked if that wish was concerning them, Hareton shook his head: *Nay, Nelly said he'll not trouble himself how we go on together, anymore*—

—as now Hareton sets aside his spade, relieved, when she calls out *Mr. Heathcliff is back, he spoke to me! But he looked so different*—

How?

And how is she to explain that smile Mr. Heathcliff gave her? Narrow and dry and white, delighted and strange, as if he gazed at her from a very great height, or from a very deep hole; was it a smile, or a baring of teeth? Yet he seemed *Almost cheerful—no, almost nothing, very much excited, and wild and glad!*

Night-walking amuses him, says Ellen, as if careless of Mr. Heathcliff's doings, contradicting herself at once by adding *It's not right to wander out of doors, in this moist season,* then hurrying to follow Mr. Heathcliff into the house, to remonstrate with him as she always does, Ellen wishes to tell them all what they must do.

And Hareton watches as if he too might follow, then looks to her and bends back to his spade, as *Ellen,* she says, loosening the roots, the grasping dirt, *Ellen says we ought not vex him*—

—yet should she tell Hareton the rest of what Ellen told her, yesterday in the kitchen, when he and Joseph were out in the sheepfold? That Mr. Heathcliff is in a peculiar humor, talking dreadful nonsense, Ellen said, of forgetting to breathe and needing to remind his heart to beat, insisting that he does not fear death, giving unchristian directions of how he is to be buried? Should she say that she herself has observed, this last long week, the way the candle flames writhe and bend toward Mr. Heathcliff, absent of any breeze, and the fire too when he stands before it? Should she say that a spot in the hallway smelled so strongly of heather that it almost made her dizzy, but the heather will not bloom again for months, or that the door to her mother's room stands wide open, close it and walk away, walk back and it stands open again, and the panels of the box bed always open too, as if to invite entrance, and silent rest? Does Ellen see none of these things? Or seeing, dismiss them, refuse their reality, Ellen too acts differently these days, almost as if she is worried, not for Mr. Heathcliff but for herself—

—but why say to Hareton any of these things? without being sure of their meaning, for good or ill? Hareton is worried enough for Mr. Heathcliff. So instead she gives him a smile in hopes of rousing his own, and says, for it is equally true, *Mr. Heathcliff is glad of something. Perhaps he's had some good news.*

Where should news come from? He's said naught to me. Well, Nelly will see to him, as if to convince them both that the matter is only of taking meals again and sleeping; he digs his spade deeper into the squared plot of quiet earth, the new green life, and *It will be a fine garden,* he says, *once it's grown.*

At dinner Mr. Heathcliff appears at table, looking worn, his hands trembling as he accepts a full plate from Ellen's hands—*I've neither cold nor fever, Nelly, and I'm ready to do justice to the food you give me*—before his attention is taken by the window—she sees it too, or nearly, that sudden shadow in the garden, no one is there to cast a shadow—and he drops his fork and knife to hurry outside. Minutes pass, he does not return, Hareton rises—*I'll ask why he won't dine*—but when Hareton steps in back in, alone, she asks, though knowing the answer, *Is he coming?*

Nay, but he did seem rare pleased. And he bid me be off to you, one hand brief and sweet to her shoulder, *he wondered how I could want the company of anybody else.*

Ellen sets that dinner plate on the fender to keep warm, but it stays uneaten and untouched, though Mr. Heathcliff finally returns, smiling, to sit at table alone—rousing more of Ellen's nervous murmurs to her: *He's talking nonsense again, I can hardly make it all out! He says he's on the threshold of hell or heaven, just three steps away, he says he has his eyes on it—*

What does he see?

—and he says you and Hareton must keep away from him altogether, now.

And when Ellen, still determined, carries him a late supper dish, she turns back almost at once, as if something in the room—Mr. Heathcliff? Or someone else?—frightens her away, calling hurriedly for Joseph, *The master wishes you to take him a light, and rekindle the fire.* Yet Joseph too goes in then directly out, clattering the fire shovel and the supper tray, saying to Ellen, though all can hear, *T'master's up to bed now, says he wants nowt till morning.*

Tonight there will be no reading lesson, neither she nor Hareton can summon the concentration: Hareton hunching by the chimney, hands tight between his knees—Hareton alone of them all has love to goad his worry, Hareton looks up again and again as if Mr. Heathcliff might reappear and reassure them—until finally she clasps his hand, warm to her cold, then rises for the stairs, for bed, though she knows she will not sleep—

—finding as she climbs that the air upstairs has thickened, as if weighted by wind or whispers, and the door to her mother's room is firmly closed. But as she passes, it opens, on a muttering inside, no words, no voice she knows: and on its threshold, the room unlit beyond one windowside candle, is Mr. Heathcliff in his shirtsleeves, his glad wild gaze seeing, what? beyond her? beyond life? Mr. Heathcliff the living bridge to her mother—

—and she feels it, that presence, stranger and stronger now than it has ever been, her mother's presence, her mother's ghost, will Mr. Heathcliff speak to her now, it seems he will speak to her now—

—but all he says is *Catherine*

—and then his hand is on the door, he closes the door and she retreats into her own room, the air thick there too as if in the last moments before a storm, and sits upon her bed, watching the door and listening, listening, waiting to hear.

At breakfast, Ellen is in a brisk and agitated temper, but Ellen does not mention Mr. Heathcliff beyond instructing them to *Get your meal before the master comes down, he's lying late.* So she and Hareton take their tea and milk and oatcakes to sit beneath the trees, Hareton half-lying on the grass, she watching the pale scudding clouds and the wheeling lapwings, until she says, *I wish to live here always, don't you?*

Aye, but—you don't pine for the t'Grange? Nelly says—Nelly says, someday you'll shift there.

No, she says. *We won't.*

The long day passes like hourglass sand, everyone attuned to the silence from the room above: Hareton keeps his work within hailing distance of the yard; Joseph spews dire opinions on the fate of the unchurched and unsaved; Ellen blisters her thumb as she boils the potatoes to sludge; and she pages through another book for their lessons, barely seeing what she reads, a swarm of words, a blur of pictures—

—until Mr. Heathcliff steps rapid into the kitchen, his eyes bloodshot, hair slick with sweat—she has seen that fevered look before, her father had it, and Linton, toward the end—and *Come, Nelly*, he says. *I want someone by me.*

But Ellen shelters behind the table, behind the chair where she sits, Ellen is plainly disturbed—*Mr. Heathcliff, your manner is too fearsome for me to sit alone with you!* which makes Mr. Heathcliff laugh, a dry laugh like dead leaves in a breeze, he turns her way instead and says *Will you come? I'll not hurt you. Though to you I've made myself worse than the devil.*

What she sees in his eyes she can put no name to, but there is no hate there nor challenge, she starts to rise but Ellen clamps a hand to her shoulder, forces her to sit again and *Well,* Mr. Heathcliff says, *there's one who won't shrink from my company—By God! she's relentless. It's too much for flesh and blood, even mine—*

—and he is gone again, back to her mother's room, where again they can hear the mutters and moans, endearments or blasphemies, hours of this until Hareton, unable to bear a minute more, mounts the stairs to knock, then rattle at the door—*He's locked hisseln in!*—then rides the mare hard to Gimmerton to fetch the doctor, while Ellen searches in vain for the extra key. But Dr. Kenneth can find no entry either: at his knock, Mr. Heathcliff says through the door that he is better, and that they must all go to hell.

Yet when Dr. Kenneth departs, Hareton stays stubborn by that door—*I'll not leave him*—while Ellen is more agitated still, urging Hareton to come down and rest, then ordering him: *Go down, Mr. Hareton, at once! You'll do yourself harm if you stay—*

You must not trouble Hareton now, she says; she knows what troubles Hareton most, she knows what it is to lose a father. *Let him be, Ellen.*

And if Mr. Hareton should fall ill, too, Miss? What's to do then! Ellen standing before her with arms akimbo, sharp with that authority she has spent all her life enforcing—

—but oh, her life has changed, she has changed, so *Let him be,* she says, staring at Ellen. *Nelly.*

When finally Hareton trudges down, they sit close together on the settle, watching the fire, until he falls into an unhappy doze, his head on her shoulder, the dogs restless, panting, pacing from the windows to the doors. Joseph enters, mouth already working to produce some hateful pronouncement, but her stern pointing finger sends Joseph up the garret ladder without a word. And where is Ellen, now? Not in the kitchen, Ellen is elsewhere, Ellen is plainly afraid; of Mr. Heathcliff? Or something else?

Her mind forms the word without saying it aloud: *Mother.*

Hours pass. It begins to rain, a drenching rain.

Mother.

And this time there is no odor of heather, the air does not thicken, the fire does not flicker or dim—but all at once she feels, as fully and truly as she feels Hareton's sleeping body beside her own, a presence there in the room, unknowable, living and wild, convincing beyond any need for belief: her mother has come back to this place that was her home, her mother is here—

—and her heart lifts, her eyes fill with tears, but not for grief—

Mother.

—and she sleeps, though she does not know it till she wakes: the rain has ended, the sun is up and shining, the kitchen lattice is open on the damp fecund air of the garden. And Ellen is there, looking weary and relieved, Joseph is there, Joseph is saying *You're t'master now, lad,* to Hareton staring up from the settle with the bewilderment of an orphaned child.

The evening of the funeral she spends alone, wearing the dress she wore for her father and for Linton, a simple mourning dress, her curls combed back. She has banished Joseph and his cruel psalms of joy into the stables, as Ellen and Hareton rode off with the coffin, Hareton still in tears—all night he sat in weeping vigil by the box bed, kissing the clay-cold bristled cheek, pressing the hand that, Ellen said, had stiffened on the windowsill; Mr. Heathcliff's eyes, Ellen said, were hard to close, *It was work to make him decent to view!* Ellen also said that *Mr. Heathcliff wished only myself and Mr. Hareton to attend his burying,* giving her a sideways look. *We must abide by his wishes, Miss, no matter how unorthodox.*

She moves quietly through the darkening rooms of the house, her house, her home and Hareton's, not unhappy, not frightened; it is so quiet she can hear the murmur of the beck as it winds toward Gimmerton, its unending flow. In her mother's room, the door unlocked and now unmoving, she sees that the box bed panels have been closed, the window hasped; she opens it wide. The May moon has risen in the sweep of lavender sky, flower moon, milk moon, hare's moon, mother's moon.

H. and I shall go to Crags at moonrise

What would they see, she and Hareton, if they went to Penistone Crags tonight?

Soon she hears the slowing hoofbeats, the wagon rolling into the courtyard, they are back from the burying. Joseph stumps out to take the horses, as Ellen alights in her mourning bonnet and tasselled black shawl, and *No minister!* Ellen says, *not one prayer said over him! It will be a sorry scandal, the whole neighborhood will talk. And the two coffins—*

—as Hareton pauses at the doorway like a stranger, his clean coat clotted now with graveside sod: Hareton Earnshaw, his name is above that door

—*but it was his wish! So we must pray, ourselves, and hope that Mr. Heathcliff will lie at peace.*

She takes Hareton's hand, grimed too with grass and grave dirt, and *He is at peace,* she says, pressing his hand to her heart. *He's rare pleased.*

Eleven

Hareton's tears

they fell like dew on whinstone, on that body by the window in the empty room, its hand reaching, cut by the lattice, its blood already ceased, its joy begun

Heathcliff once told Nelly *Twenty times a day I covet Hareton, I'd have loved the lad had he been someone else! But I think he's safe from her love*

no one is safe from love

and my daughter and Hareton have found it so, they will live at the Heights, inherit and lay balm to the lives we would have led—our children, together

they are fine children

Edgar do you see?

Nelly plots still to direct them, still thinks she may, as if they were hers to manage—Nelly means to establish them at the Grange, seeks to be the mistress of the Grange in all but name. but my Catherine will teach her presently her right place, my Catherine is mistress now, mistress of the Heights

though Nelly seeks to flee the Heights, she told that stranger tenant *I don't like being left by myself in this grim house, now, I don't like being out in the dark*

Nelly fears us

she should

her fear cooked the food she tried again and again to force upon Heathcliff in his last days living, *you must be hungry, rambling all night! your dinner is here, why won't you get it? eat and drink while it is hot! suppose you persevered in your obstinate fast, and died?* because the change he spoke of was coming, he told her plain enough, *My soul's bliss kills my body—I'm too happy, and yet I'm not happy enough*

he knew what he must do, but not how it might be done

that was my work

calling, insisting, demanding, that was his food and drink

and the last night at the Crags—his first time to the fairy-kirk since I died, our marriage made anew in bog mud and salt sweat, his body hard against the rock, the moon and the moths as white as a bridal train, he felt me in every breath and shudder, he knew me, *no one can ever part us now*

and stumbling back to the Heights in the dawn as if he had just left Eden, the worlds shifting and he in both, sallow and smiling, shivering like a tight-stretched twist of gut, breathing fast as a cat

because the body fights to live

I remember

and as his own body dwindled he saw me more and more plainly, he forced that dwindling so he could see more, as with every seeing moment all else around him became less real—*How to leave my property! I wish I could annihilate it from the face of the earth*—finally he knew all that foolishness for what it was! that vengeful accumulation, that vicious waste of time

and Nelly preaching to him about ministers and the Bible, as if she were Joseph, as if she believed in any of such herself! *Strange happiness, master! You have lived a selfish unchristian life, how unfit you will be for Heaven*—

I tell you I have nearly attained my heaven

gazing to me as he said it, there in the house where we lived our sweetest days, barely separated, shimmering in his vision, in his straining dying eagerness, praying to me in his last words, *By God! she's relentless*

I said I would not rest until he was with me, and I did not, I never did

I journeyed for him

I fought for him

I won him at the last

once, as children, we sat to watch a pearly moth struggle into life in one of the garret windows—his last struggle was the same, he was born as that moth was born, his life beating free from the chrysalis of his heart, there by the window, in our bed, his face washed with the rain

once he wished us to mingle our bodies in their coffins, let the moss and the heather cover them as they dissolved together into earth—it was the best mingling he could fathom—but now we have a better, more ecstatic communion, *we* are the moss and heather, the thistles and the thorns, the beck, the blood and the body's fluids, the moving shadows beneath the Nab, the streaks of light where no light should be, the sounds the horses shy from in the stable, we make the dogs bark, we make Joseph hide his candle and shiver in his garret on rainy nights, we frighten the folk in Gimmerton who swear to one another that we walk, we make Nelly stumble and hurry in the dark, we make Hareton look up and Catherine look thoughtful

we are terror and love

Nelly put her question to that stranger, *Do you believe such people are happy in the other world, Mr. Lockwood? I'd give a great deal to know*

now she knows

we saw that stranger stop on his way back to his other, smaller world, the Grange and London, the spinning earth, to stare at our graves, Heathcliff's and mine, and Edgar's on my left, as if seeking our ending there—the kirk itself is dead, slates fall off the roof into the grass, we broke the windows—he imagined us as quiet and sleeping

sleep is for the body

death is for the body

surely you, and everybody, have a notion that there is or should be an existence of yours beyond you

we have ours now

bliss upon bliss upon bliss

whatever our souls are made of, his and mine are the same

Acknowledgements

Thanks to Leza Cantoral for the spark and CLASH for the home and Christopher Schelling for always knowing what comes next. Deepest thanks to Emily Brontë, unparalleled writer, innovator, and queen.

Kathe Koja

Kathe Koja writes and creates immersive fiction in novels, short stories, and performance events in various media. She has won the Shirley Jackson Award, Bram Stoker Award, Locus Award, and was a finalist for the Philip K. Dick and World Fantasy awards, among many others. *Wuthering Heights* is her favorite novel.

Also by Kathe Koja

Also by Clash Books

Everything The Darkness Eats
Eric LaRocca

The Body Harvest
Michael Seidlinger

Flowers From The Void
Gianni Washington

The Black Tree Atop The Hill
Karla Yvette

Helena
Claire Smith

Invaginies
Joe Koch

Cenote City
Monique Quintana

Charcoal
Garrett Cook

WE PUT THE LIT IN LITERARY
clashbooks.com

 @clashbooks  @clashbooks /clashbooks

Email
clashmediabooks@gmail.com